THE MERRY WIDOW
A REGENCY STANDALONE NOVELLA

TRISHA FUENTES

ARDENT ARTIST BOOKS

The Merry Widow
Copyright © 2019-2024 by Trisha Fuentes
All rights reserved.

Book Cover and formatting provided by Trisha Fuentes
https://bit.ly/m/trishafuentes

No part of this book may be reproduced in any form or by any electronic or mechanical means, including information storage and retrieval systems, without written permission from the author, except for the use of brief quotations in a book review.

ISBN: 979-8-3302-2302-2 (Paperback)

Published by
Ardent Artist Books
www.ardentartistbooks.com

ABOUT ARDENT ARTIST BOOKS

Ardent Artist Books was established in 2008.

We publish modern and historical romances once a month!

For a complete list of our published books and books in development, please visit our website at:

https://ardentartistbooks.com/free-downloads

FREE DOWNLOAD
Updated Monthly!

Follow us on YouTube to see what new stories are on the horizon!

https://www.youtube.com/theardentartist

Like, Subscribe & Comment

LET'S CONNECT!

Fuel your love of fiction with exclusive content and captivating insights from Ardent Artist Books. Whether you crave the thrill of modern narratives or the timeless elegance of historical fiction, our newsletter delivers a curated selection straight to your inbox.

Plus, as a welcome gift, receive a FREE downloadable eBook:

"The Family Fix"

https://mailchi.mp/567874a61a56/aab-landing-page

The Merry Widow

PROLOGUE

Lucy looked across at the older Gentlemen and surveyed his countenance. He had mentioned several times during the course of dinner that he was single or unmarried and then rested eyes on her.

He was fashionable and plain-featured but he did have an air about him that intrigued her. He was self-assured and she did find that quality most desirable.

He was not titled, but did own a townhome in London she heard him say. He was only there in Surrey to visit his friends he mentioned, for a few days, then he had to head back.

When he laughed, his eyes lit up which caused hers to sparkle with the possibly of excitement he might show her in bed.

Yes, he would be in her bed.

She knew so the moment he rested eyes on her divide above her bodice when they were introduced.

He was interested in a quick *romp*, and so was she.

It had been a month since her husband last touched her.

Only four weeks since she felt any sort of intimacy.

She was alone and lonely and yearned for carnal knowledge.

Would the Gentleman deliver?

Lucy could only hope...

CHAPTER 1

DORKING, 1818

THREE MONTH'S AFTER

Lucy stood over her husband's grave. It was an enormous marble memorial with carved lettered etchings:

HERE LIES
THE EARL OF MOWBRAY
BELOVED HUSBAND, FATHER AND SON
LORD HORACE MOWBRAY
1748 - 1818

Bowing her head down, she recalled the last time she'd seen him, spoke to him, touched him. Her heart hurt because she was lonely and missed his companionship and longed to be a couple once more. She had never felt more isolated than she did so at present. Surrounded by household staff was not the same as being enclosed in someone's arms.

She bent over and laid the bouquet of roses she cut hours before down on the marble ledge, and looked up and across at others gathering around nearby gravesites. One man in particular caught her attention, and she stepped to the side of the memorial to view him more clearly.

Several yards away, he stood over a single grave, he was alone and had not taken off his hat to pay his respects to whomever was buried there. He intrigued her only because he was tall, fashionable, most likely Gentry and handsome.

His dark features only enhanced his good looks and Lucy's curiosity stirred. Her eyes bounced from him back to her husband's memorial, and grimaced for she knew she would be disrespectful if she did bed another man so soon ... *well*, so soon after the last man she bed.

She was still young, only twenty years old and she yearned for *desire*, to be *wanted*, and to be *fulfilled*. The emptiness in and around her estate was solitude she no longer wanted to partake in.

Lucy raised her eyes to the Gentlemen who now

looked towards her standing. He stood motionless and stared back. The exchange between them was intense and Lucy felt her blood begin to boil. He turned back towards his own gravestone, and then looked up quickly across at her.

Lucy continued to stand by her husband's memorial when all of a sudden, the Gentlemen stepped forward and began to walk towards her locale.

Her eyes grew wide when he drew closer. While he introduced himself, the heat in his eyes alone spoke to her eagerness to know him further.

"Mr. Colin Bishop, Madam," he said with a bow. "I apologize, if I am intruding."

Lucy let go a small smile. "No, sir, you are not intruding," she expressed, with a curtsey, "Lady Mowbray."

Mr. Bishop smiled and then dropped his eyes down the length of her black dress and coat, and then raised them to her fiery red hair. "I come here once a year," he relayed, gazing across at the splendor, "to visit my wife, deceased now for these past twenty years. This is the first time our paths have crossed."

Lucy gazed into his welcoming blue eyes, "My husband, Mr. Bishop, gone now three months."

Mr. Bishop nodded his head congenially and walked around her to view the carvings on the memorial.

Reading the epitaph, he turned to gaze at her again, "Newly arrived; you must miss him dearly."

Lucy felt her heart beat escalating, "Yes, very much so."

They stood together an arm's length away but the magnetism between them was undeniable.

Mr. Bishop's mouth opened slightly as he dropped his eyes to her lips, and if he could read her thoughts, he uttered, "My coach is behind the church."

Lucy looked deep into his eyes and then grabbed his crooked elbow to walk with him as they traipsed across the churchyard towards his coach.

It was a rather large coach, a five seater at best and Lucy sat next to him and then laid her head down on his chest to hear his own heart beating swiftly. Sniffling for a few seconds, Mr. Bishop raised her chin, and then brought his open mouthed kiss down on her lips and tasted her deeply.

After all, it was what her body was craving for … to be touched, to be wanted, to be … *filled.*

Deep kisses quickly turned erotic, as the two of them began to discard their coats inside the small confine. Darting towards her neck, Mr. Bishop bussed his tongue and kisses down her skin, and towards the opening of her bosom where he pulled down her bodice with his teeth to suckle and lick at one exposed nipple. Lucy arched her back on the coach seat in arousal, and then watched Mr. Bishop as he knelt down, pulled up her skirts, and rooted her again and again, furnishing her with what her body cried out for. Throwing her head back in exhilaration, she surged forward making sure she could feel every bit of him and closed her eyes at last to feel her temporary bit of rapture.

CHAPTER 2

FIVE MONTH'S AFTER

Lucy walked around the tailor's store and ran her fingers across the many ready-made dresses and gowns he had on display. Pinks, whites, blues of every shade excited her for the day she would be out of mourning and able to wear everyday attire again.

"Mr. Ainsworth," Lucy called out for his attention.

Mr. Henry Ainsworth gazed up from his fabric cutting, "Yes, Lady Mowbray?"

"I rather liked the dress you made me before my husband passed, could we layer black tulle over the silk?" She asked, walking closer to his locale. He had been at a cutting table, with men's suit fabric thrown across its wide flat surface.

"The red silk? The empire?" He asked, jotting down the order on a small sheet of paper.

Lucy nodded her head, "Yes, I rather like that pattern. Would you be able to make me another?"

"In black, Madam?" He asked, innocently.

Lucy looked at him more clearly. He wasn't a bad looking fellow for a working man in his late forties. A little taller than herself, his hair grayed at the temples, and his blue eyes pierced through her curiosity as they slightly dropped down to her bosom. Lucy took note of the indiscretion and asked, "You have any appointments this week, Mr. Ainsworth?"

Mr. Ainsworth lowered his fountain pen, "Only a few, I am quite busy the following week though."

"Any appointments today?" Lucy asked, impishly gazing away from his weird look.

He tilted his head, "Why no, you are my last appointment."

Lucy let go a gamine smile and dropped her eyes to his lips. It had been a month since her tryst in the coach at the graveyard with Mr. Bishop, and Lucy yearned for *desire*, to be *wanted*, and to be *fulfilled*. "Do you fit for undergarments, Mr. Ainsworth?"

He squinted his eyes at her and looked up at the

ceiling, "Never had that request before, Madam, you would be my first."

Lucy did not look his way and fingered some nearby wool on a bolt, "Silk undergarments, Mr. Ainsworth, in a lacy French design."

"French?" He asked, blushing.

Lucy knew Mr. Ainsworth had never been married. He had been making her dresses and ball gowns since she first married Lord Mowbray, and she knew he might be as lonely as she was at present. "Will you measure me?"

He raised his eyebrows at her request, and immediately grabbed his measuring tape.

Lucy stepped forward and dropped her coat to the floor. With her arms stretched out straight at either side, Mr. Ainsworth began to slowly guide the tape across her shoulders with gentle touches, and breathtaking innuendo.

Lucy raised her eyes towards his and Mr. Ainsworth licked his lips. Dropping her eyes down to his pucker, she wrapped her arms around his neck but did not kiss him ... *yet*. "I am lonely," she whispered by his ear. "I ask for nothing, want nothing but prudence in this matter."

Mr. Ainsworth dropped his measuring tape to the floor and then wrapped his own arms around her body and pulled her closer. "I am lonely too," he voiced tenderly, leaning in to give her a small kiss across her lips.

He wasn't lovely to look at like Mr. Bishop was, but a means to an end and Lucy did not want to lose the opportunity. She brought his body closer into hers, and darted in towards his lips and kissed him. He was a good kisser and Lucy was glad for it, for Mr. Ainsworth treated her lips greedily as he broke away from her skin only to buss his touches across her neck and shoulder. Walking her backwards towards his high cutting table, he pushed her wanton body up against the stiffness off the edge, and lifted her body up so that she could sit slightly on its rim. Wrapping her arms around his backside, she helped him unbutton his pantaloons, and pull them down to his ankles. Feeling his two hands up and around her upper thighs, she aided him in lifting up her skirts, and pushed forward to receive a fullness unsurpassed. He was thick, long and excited as he pumped her way too quickly for her to gain any sort of leverage in satisfying herself. Leaning away from his nearing body which wanted to lie limp across hers in culmination, she began to move her hips, and finally met her own selfish desire and brief lustful end by latching onto him still thickset inside her.

CHAPTER 3

SURREY, 1819

ONE YEAR A WIDOW

Lady Lucy Mowbray woke up at first light peeking in through her curtains. Alone in her king-sized bed, she felt listless and abandoned and thought about the last time she bed a man.

He was a tailor, and one of her husband's longtime friends and forthwith one of hers. He was older than she was, by twenty-two years, but it did not matter much for the man was sinful by his breadth and sent her home with a smile.

Her husband of three years, Lord Horace Mowbray had been fifty years older than she, and was buried at St. Martin's in Dorking. A widow at twenty-one years of age, Lucy was now titled and a very wealthy woman, with her husband's will leaving her ten thousand a year, their grand estate he purchased as a wedding gift, horses, stables, three carriages, a barn and twenty servants all at her beck and call.

Her husband used to affectionately call her *Marigold*, for the color of her crimson hair and confessed to her once that her hair was the reason he fell in love with her. He bucked the naysayers to marry her, especially his older children by his first marriage, Lord Horace Mowbray, II, in his fifties, his wife, Lady Marjory, and his sister, Lady Felicity, a spinster, in her early forties. Her husband's youngest son, Lord Arthur Mowbray, who had been seven years older than she, was once a student at Cambridge and now a practicing solicitor.

Lucy had been a housemaid for Lord Mowbray on their estate just outside of London. Lavernham Manor was his ancestral home, a residency where his children and grandchildren currently resided in and where Lucy was no longer welcome.

She never did once give into Lord Mowbray's advances when she was a housemaid, not until their wedding night, but Horace II nor his sister Felicity ever believed otherwise. They did catch her once or twice, sitting on his lap and feeding him strawberry's though, something her husband cherished immensely and would later tell her so in confidence.

Nevertheless, she did have genuine feelings for the old man, he took care of her, sheltered her, clothed and fed her and occasionally would like to give her a sponge bath. Watching his eyes fill with heat gave her pleasure and she fully expected to be satisfied in return, but he always fell short. His hands were cold, his kisses on her skin were brittle and harsh, and instead of suckling her breasts in rapture, he bit them and sometimes left them bruised.

She would miss him all the same, marriage to him meant constant companionship, for the only close friendships she had at present were those of servitude; her lady's maid, Miss Mary Hurndale and her head housekeeper, Mrs. Abigail Thatchwood.

Her husband had been gone from this earth twelve months, and Lucy never felt more alone than she did waking up early to watch the sun rise. A new day meant families were getting out of bed, children were being woken up from their slumber, servants were making breakfast for the family and their tea.

She was by oneself most days, with the occasional invite to a dinner party, or one of her husband's longtime friends calling on her to see how she was holding up.

Having only showed grief once at the burial service for her husband, Lucy always wondered why she was not further devastated by his departure. He was a good man, a happy sort of Gentry, who was amiable and pleasant and treated her like a princess, and since he was a man of good character, Lucy treated him like a king. How his children did not see how much they cared for one another was unfathomable. Their mother had passed twenty years before, Lucy was a baby when she died, how did they believe that their father was being unfaithful?

Horace II and his wife, Marjory were the worst sort of lot; conceited, self-centered and snobbish. Felicity was a little bit more amiable, having conversed with her once or twice about trivial subjects of conversation, but at least she did not sneer when she walked into a room. Then there was the youngest son, Arthur. She remembered Arthur before he left for Cambridge, he was quite the scamp with his teasing ways. She remembered he did give her a kiss on her wedding day, a small peck, a gesture of acceptance which she believed might be an open door to welcoming her into the family, not the opposition she later received during her marriage to their father.

But she did try ... she always did try, but every time she would make an attempt to be gracious, the family would bat her down like a fruit fly.

CHAPTER 4

The one thing that Lucy always wanted was children. She desperately longed for them and fully expected her marriage to bear fruit. She was seventeen, and a virgin when she bed Lord Mowbray the very first time. She once thought she was with child, but a false alarm, and later learned, just her nerves.

The doctor told her that the age differences between herself and her husband might not bear any issue, that Lord Mowbray may be sterile, and no longer able to father a child. But she did have hope, and she did try. Seducing her husband, fondling him under the covers until he was hard enough so she could ride him for seed. But with each passing month, hopes diminished until one day, Lord Mowbray stopped breathing altogether.

They were in bed, having just arrived home from a

dinner party and were dressed for sleep. Lucy had been lying on her back, in her nightgown talking about the singer at the party when her husband reached over and lowered her gown down to her breast.

The next thing she knew was her husband forcing himself over her, lying flat across her midriff, and pumping at her legs to find entrance. Realizing the urgency, Lucy opened up her thighs while her husband bit down on her breast and felt him enter ... *then wince* ... then without warning, fall limp across her body. He felt like heavy weight on top of her when she mistaken his idleness for finishing too soon. She whispered his name several times and then became frightened from his nonresponse. Pushing him off of her, he rolled over with an open stare that still haunted her to this day.

"What do you wish to wear this evening, Madame?" Mary, Lucy's lady's maid asked, while shuffling through her wardrobe.

Lucy glanced over at Mary, "Oh how I wish I could wear pink, but I am obligated to wear this wretched black. One more week of wearing this cheerless color and I am free to wear whatever I want."

Mary gave her employer a small smile, "My lord was good to you though."

Lucy nodded her head in agreement, "He was, indeed."

Mary noticed that her employer grew melancholy by the moment, "This gown always looks good on you."

Lucy glanced over at Mary now holding the black silk gown with black flowers embroidered into its tulle, the one she had the dressmaker sew especially for her. "That will do," she said, glancing back to her dresser mirror. She was getting ready for a dinner party that included her so-called relatives. Her husband's children would all be in attendance, and she was not looking forward to seeing them.

The last time that she did see them was at the solicitor's office during the reading of the will. Felicity stormed out, crying and carrying on, Horace II, shouting off the top of his lungs, roaring his frustration at how their father passed. *It was embarrassing,* they all said and admitted. Knowing their father took his last breath during sexual relations? Even Arthur, having known to not really saying much, had much to say that evening and thundered out as well.

Mary laid the gown down on top of her bed, and then ambled over to Lucy who had been trying to brush her own hair out.

"Allow me," she voiced, grabbing the brush and taking a piece of Lucy's long, fiery red hair into her hands and polishing it out. Curling it around her fingers, she placed it to her head, and then pinned it in place with flowered pins and repeated the action until Lucy's head was full of curls joined together by white rose pedaled pins. "There," she announced, gazing at her employer in the mirror.

Lucy turned her head left then right and admired herself in the reflection. She was still very beautiful, with fiery red hair, bright blue eyes, and with her wealth now, a dangerous mixture. "Perfect," she let go, smiling at Mary in her reflection.

"Will the second be there?" Mary asked, putting in Lucy's ear bobs.

"Yes," Lucy uttered, rolling her eyes, "as well as Lady Felicity and the youngest."

"Is he back from Cambridge?" Mary asked, applying powder and rouge to Lucy's cheeks.

Lucy watched Mary as she livened up her pale skin, "Yes, graduated last year and has been practicing law in Portsmouth and visiting Lavernham Manor with the rest of them."

"I recall when the youngest once tried to kiss me," Mary smiled, adjusting a pin in Lucy's hair.

Lucy gazed up at her lady's maid. Miss Mary

Hurndale had been a housemaid with her at Lavernham. Both the same age, Lucy insisted she come to work for her at the Mowbray Estate as her lady's maid. Not as beautiful as Lucy, Mary did hold a certain attractiveness and could see why Arthur would try and make an advance towards her. "And? Did he succeed?"

Mary shook her head, "I pushed him away."

Lucy shook her head too, "Then I presume he must have tried with someone else. I do recall him being quite mischievous, he did try to converse with me once or twice."

"And devilishly handsome too! Heavens me, I do not know how I made it out of that closet with my clothes still on," Mary laughed, raising her eyes towards her employer's.

Lucy sniggered with her as well, "Handsome, you say? Somehow, I do not remember."

"That is because you only had eyes for his father," Mary proclaimed, smiling down at her sitting in the chair.

Lucy glared at her reflection. *Eyes for his father*, she thought. *She did care for Horace, but never truly loved him. She never knew what it was like to be in love, and wondered now if she ever was. If she was, it no longer mattered, he was dead and she was alive. Alive, to do whatever she wanted.*

CHAPTER 5

FRIMLEY MANOR

All eyes rested on Lucy the moment she walked into the parlor for drinks.

Frimley Manor was owned by Mr. and Mrs. Stuart Frimley, longtime friends of her husband's and Mrs. Frimley, an acquaintance of Lucy's. They only invited her to dine with them when the Mowbray family were in attendance and on this night, they were all there.

Horace II gave her a sneer and raised his nose in the air the moment she entered the span. His father's child bride had always been a thorn stuck in his shoe. He loathed her simply because his father would make a fool of himself while in her presence. Falling all over himself the moment she walked into a room; serving her, fetching things for her, practically feeding her with a spoon. His father was reduced to nothing but a dunderhead while in her company, and he admired his father for his good sense, knowledge of business and maintenance of his wealth. Being the heir to the Earldom of Mowbray, he was left with nothing but a small annual income, and their ancestral home after the reading of his father's will, no doubt half his inheritance bequeathed to her. Rewritten and influenced by that harlot who somehow captured his father under her spell. "The crimson opportunist has made an appearance," he said under his breath towards his wife.

Lady Marjory Mowbray, raised her eyebrows, and leaned into her husband, "And she had the impertinence of attending without a companion."

Lady Felicity Mowbray, sipped her Madeira and watched in silence as her step-mother acknowledged everyone in the room. Stopping by to say hello to every Gentleman in attendance like a bee buzzing from flower to flower. How she had the audacity to continue to show herself in public, when she should be at home in solitude and mourning was inexplicable. Felicity dropped her eyes down the length of Lucy, chipping away at her brazenness to show herself at this social gathering, unaccompanied. Her father buried and her step-mother out and about, smiling with her flirtatious behavior. "Has she no shame?" Felicity let go, shaking her head.

Lucy finished acknowledging everyone in assembly, everyone but the three who would be the most important. Gathering up her courage, she slowly walked over towards them all standing together in a clump. "Lord and Lady Mowbray, how nice it is to see you again," she voiced sweetly, trying to gain eye contact with at least one of them. "Lady Felicity," she acknowledged with a small curtsy.

It was Arthur who finally spoke up and walked around from his three bitter relatives. Bowing his head to her first, he said, "Nice to see you well, step-mother."

Lucy tore her eyes away from their iciness, and rested her glare now on Lord Arthur Mowbray. Tall and fashionable, she could see why Mary declared him devilishly handsome, for Arthur grew up confidant and good-humored, unlike his older siblings. Dark brown hair, like Horace II and Felicity, but with green-brown eyes that only enhanced his good looks. Lucy smiled at him and bore into those hazel eyes, "Thank you, Lord Mowbray, it is always nice to see *you*."

They stood there together, smiling at one another when Horace II spoke up to break the drawing power they generated between them. "You came alone, Miss Lucy?"

Lucy gazed over at Horace II. Addressing her informally and no longer acknowledging her title was a direct insult to her person. But she wasn't going to allow her late husband's horrid children get the best of her. "Not staying very long, Lord Mowbray, and besides, the sun still shines on my mourning dress."

Horace II grimaced, and then swallowed the rest of his wine. "You are unwelcome here," he whispered low by her ear.

Lucy swallowed his threatening tone, "I was invited this night to dine with Mr. and Mrs. Frimley."

"No doubt an oversight," Felicity added next, reducing her frown to a thin line.

"Step-mother," Arthur said with a sigh, "would you care to take a turn of the room?"

Lucy tore her eyes away from Horace II's repulsive presence, and grabbed at Arthur's forearm immediately, "Yes, thank you." Trying to calm her heart down she tried desperately to hold back the tears that were now forming at the back of her eyes.

"Breathe," Arthur softly said, smiling at everyone while they both gradually walked the drinking parlor.

Lucy swallowed hard before she voiced, "How can one breathe when your insolent brother sucks the very air from the room."

Arthur let go a small laugh. She surprised him actually with her congenial quality, having never truly sat down and had a conversation with her before. He decided to rescue her after that terrible display of unsympathetic accord from his siblings. He felt sorry for her, and felt no one should have to endure feeling like an outcast. "Once you get to know my brother, he can be quite charming."

"Charming?" Lucy laughed out loud, bringing attention towards the two walking further away from everyone. "Where does he hide this supposed charm? His toes?"

Arthur laughed out loud as well, eyeing several guests turning their heads. "His fingernails," he quickly quipped, "from time to time you can find him admiring them."

Lucy let out a hoot, which caused every guest to fully gaze at the couple. Trying to contain her smile, Lucy raised her wine glass in the air, "To Mr. and Mrs. Frimley...and bringing us together."

Every guest turned towards one another, and then turned towards Mr. and Mrs. Frimley and raised their glasses in the air.

"To Mr. and Mrs. Frimley."

CHAPTER 6

*L*ucy had been seated next to Arthur and she was glad for it. Throughout dinner, the two had ignored civil conversation and enjoyed one another's company with their own private parley, talking about everything from the subject of horses, to the London theatre to the Prince Regent. In fact, the more Lucy was in Arthur's proximity, the closer she wanted to be.

He held a hypnotic tone to his voice while he spoke, and she found herself on several instances, staring down at his lips during conversation. She was entranced by his knowledge of hunting and the sea, and was sometimes overwhelmed by his magnetic charisma. It was a good thing she was planning on leaving the party straight after dinner, for further closeness to Lord Arthur Mowbray could possibly find him in her bed.

He *would be* in her bed if she did not run away. Others were not so fortunate. She had to remind herself that Arthur was her late husband's son and therefore, strictly off limits.

Lucy grabbed her coat, gloves and handbag in a hurry from the footman and practically ran towards her carriage where her driver already had the door open for her to step into.

Once inside, she tried to calm her heart down, for she could feel her heart beginning to yearn to be back by his side. She felt her horses surge forward and her heart fell to the pit of her stomach, knowing full well she might not ever see him again.

Lucy closed her eyes and leaned her head back on the carriage bench trying desperately to alleviate the pressure now forming in her heart. *How did this happen so quickly?* She thought. *Eager to be in one's presence yet again. Longing to know him further, wondering what it felt like to kiss his lips?* She was not used to the restriction of fulfilling her immediate desire. This suppression, this restraint … it felt like a chokehold on her throat. Just then, Lucy doubled over on the bench and began to cry. It had been months since she allowed any man to graze his fingers across her skin, and she longed to be touched yet again. She hungered to be loved, and to feel love, and sobbed for the attention she once possessed from her late husband.

MOWBRAY ESTATE

Reaching her gate's at last, Lucy saw that Mary had been waiting for her at the top of the staircase as her carriage cleared the bend.

Lucy was let down by the footman and then was joined by Mary who ran down the steps to be by her side.

"Do tell me what happened," Mary requested, grabbing her employer's coat off her shoulders and walking up the steps with her.

Lucy gazed around her and at all the ears within hearing distance, "Not here."

The two women walked side by side, down the long corridor, and up the main staircase, where the two picked up speed, and ran down the hallway towards the master bedroom, giggling.

Shutting the double doors behind her, Lucy went towards her bed and threw herself backwards on top of it. "Oh Mary, I had the most wonderful night," Lucy sighed, staring up at the canopy above her posts.

Mary wandered over and then sat down on the edge. "Wonderful? Oh do tell me what happened! Was the second horrible to you again?"

Lucy nodded her head, "Yes, and so was his dreadful sister."

"I believe those two have never been truly happy," Mary voiced, reaching out and fingering the embroidery on Lucy's black mourning dress.

Lucy rolled her eyes, "I suppose you're right. Losing their mother to brain fever."

"Mrs. Thatchwood would have to stay up throughout the night just to tend to her," Mary replied, running her hands down her skirts.

"I know, I heard the stories," Lucy blinked back, bringing her hand up to her forehead.

"Awful business, caring for someone dying," Mary relayed, waving at Lucy now to stand up so she could get her out of that dress. "Turn around," she asked, circling her finger in the air.

Lucy stood up and did what was asked of her, standing at attention while someone undressed her. It was a custom she would never get used to, having been a housemaid since she was fourteen. "Had a conversation with Arthur at last."

Mary's grin grew wide, "So, was he pleasant?"

Lucy's grin grew wider, "Very much so."

Mary tilted her head at her, "How much so?"

Lucy stared into her friends eyes. Miss Mary Hurndale was the only friend she had in the world and she knew deep down she would never hurt her. "Mary?"

Mary hushed down and grabbed Lucy's hands away from her midriff, "What? What happened?"

"I can't stop thinking about him," Lucy gushed, walking over to her window and looking out at the stars. "I close my eyes and I see his face. I yearn for him to touch me, to kiss me, to embrace me in the dark and deep down I know I will *never* see him again."

Mary rushed over to be by Lucy's side and grabbed at her hand, "But he is family, surely the Mowbray's would inquire about your well-being."

Lucy laughed out loud, "I should say not!"

Mary nodded her head, "Do not say that. I believe that God has a hand in true love."

"True love?" Lucy said, taken back. "I did not admit I was in love."

"But," Mary replied, releasing her hand, "you said you yearned for him."

"*Yearned* yes," Lucy acknowledged, "but *not* love. I daresay I am in lust with Arthur and nothing more. I want his *body*, not his *heart*."

"If you feel that strongly about his body now, could not capturing his heart follow?" Mary asked, wide-eyed and smiling.

"Do not," Lucy mocked, yanking down her dress and slipping out of the skirt. "He is my late husband's youngest son. At best, I became infatuated by the resemblance."

Mary bit down on her lower lip, "Of course, that is what it was. You miss your husband."

Lucy closed her eyes and nodded her head, "It was precisely what it was."

But was it really?

CHAPTER 7

The next morning Lucy sat alone at her breakfast table, sipping her tea. She thought about what she said last night to Mary about being in *lust* and not in *love*. Tossing and turning, she thought her head would explode with trying to discern between the two sentiments. *Was she in love, or was it just lust?*

Lucy was in mid-sip when she eyed her Butler, Mr. Dunbar walking towards her.

"Pardon me, Lady Mowbray, but this was just delivered by messenger," Mr. Dunbar relayed, handing Lucy a silver tray with a letter on top of it.

Lucy reached over and grabbed the envelope, "Thank you, Mr. Dunbar, is Mary up?"

"Yes, I believe she is with Mrs. Thatchwood," Mr. Dunbar relayed.

"Call her here," Lucy instructed, fingering the letter within her hands.

"Yes, Lady Mowbray," Mr. Dunbar replied with a service bow.

Lucy waited until he left the room to gaze down at the wax seal. The familiar Mowbray *"M"* was stamped into its wax and she tore it open. Reading and gasping for air, Lucy clutched her throat in shock.

Mary had walked into the breakfast room when she spotted Lucy with her hand to her throat, "Good God, what has happened?"

Lucy shook her head and then raised her eyes towards Mary, "Lavernham Manor ... has burnt to the ground."

Mary slowly lowered her posterior to a chair, "What? How?"

"Lord Mowbray has explained there was an accident last evening with a chandelier that fell, and exploded into the curtains. When they arrived home from the Frimley's, half the manor was in flames, and the other half already burnt to the ground. The servants all tried desperately to save it, but to no avail."

Mary could not believe her ears! Lavernham's servants were all in their sixties with one, maybe two servants young enough to fetch a water pail. Lavernham

Manor was helpless in the hands of its retired servants. "What now? What are they to do?"

Lucy turned the letter over and read the rest. In shock and disbelief, she raised her eyes towards Mary's, "They are on their way *here*. Having left this morning with what is left of their belongings. He has asked to stay at Mowbray Estate in the interim of finding better lodgings."

Mary's mouth flew open wide, "How dare he insult the hand that feeds him! In the same breath, he has the nerve to ask to welcome him inside these four walls, while he rubs your face in the mud?"

Lucy swallowed her pride, "It is true, he is dishonorable. But he has three children who are also destitute, and his father would not expect me to be inhospitable."

"Oh dearest, how big your heart is," Mary quipped, shaking her head.

"Nonsense," Lucy replied, tossing the letter to the side. "It is what my husband would do for family. And believe it or not, they *are* my family."

Mary nodded her head, "Yes, I daresay they are."

Lucy stood up immediately and smoothed down her skirts, "Call Dunbar, and Mrs. Thatchwood, we must make their stay here welcome. The guest rooms must be aired out, with clean sheets and linen, and instruct the cook to order more food."

Mary nodded her head in agreement.

Lucy looked her up and down in silence and then reached over to give her friend a hug, "We must stay resilient in this examination dear friend, for we are being tested."

LUCY AND HER STAFF WELCOMED THE Mowbray's when they arrived in the middle of the night. The servants all stood in a row while Lucy and Mary were situated at the top of the stairs.

Gazing down at them as they arrived, they all appeared tired, disheveled and full of soot. It had been a long two days for them all and Lucy was sure they required rest and the nearest bed.

"Mr. Dunbar, show Lord and Lady Mowbray to their rooms," Lucy instructed, watching Horace II walk gingerly up the stairs. She then looked beyond the family, "Your servicemen, Lord Mowbray, where are they?"

He gazed around at his family, "Our carriage house did not burn down, Madame, there is ample room for them to lodge there. Our servicemen stayed behind." He then raised his eyes to hers unwilling to relent but voiced, "Thank you for your hospitality."

Lucy looked deep into his and felt something odd about his statement, "Yes, well, I do not have a valet, Sir, but my Butler, Mr. Dunbar is at your service, Lord Mowbray, anything you need, please do not hesitate to call on him."

"Thank you," Felicity said next, wiping away hair that had been dangling all around her face.

Lucy lowered her eyes to her dress, it was full of ash, stains and was torn at the hem. "Lady Felicity, Mrs. Thatchwood has been instructed to have a bath ready for you. There are clean clothes in the closet, feel free to choose any garment as your own."

Felicity gazed downwards and bit down on her lower lip, "Yes, I—I thank you."

Lucy smiled at her as she walked up through the steps and then rested eyes on Arthur who came out of the coach at last. Wearing only his white shirt, no waistcoat, pantaloons and riding boots, he appeared worn out and unrested; his hair was mussed up, and he looked like he needed a shave. He helped out Lord Mowbray's seventeen year old daughter, Rebecca, from within the coach, followed by two younger boys, Horace III, fifteen and William, thirteen.

Lucy bounced her eyes from one child to the next. It

had been several years since she'd seen Horace II's children, they did not attend her wedding nor did they come to the burial. They were kept from her sight while she was married to their grandfather, and Lucy always wondered why. Lucy stepped down to greet Arthur and gave him a welcoming smile, "Hello again."

Arthur smiled in return, "Hello … Thank you for receiving us, Madame," he said with a small bow. He then turned towards the children and reintroduced them, "May I formally introduce my niece and nephews, Lady Rebecca, Lords Horace III and his brother, William."

Lucy curtseyed to their social rank and voiced quickly, "Rooms are available for everyone to rest in. I hope you do not mind sharing a room with your younger brother, Lord Mowbray."

Horace III gave her a small smile, "No, Madame, I do not mind. I forgot how pretty you were."

Arthur leaned back and then mussed up his nephews head of hair, "It is too soon for you young man to notice such things."

"Uncle, I am fifteen and not a monk," Horace III jested, climbing up the stairs.

Lucy watched the boys with Arthur go through the door when she noticed Rebecca standing back.

"I remember when you were employed at Lavernham

as a housemaid," Rebecca uttered softly. "You used to change my bedsheets."

Lucy smiled and stepped down to her level, "And I remember you, Lady Rebecca having eyes for one of the footman."

Rebecca's face flushed pink and she covered her hands over her face, "No one was ever supposed to know that! How did *you* know?"

Lucy wrapped her arms around her shoulders as they walked up the stairs to the front door, "All females know of the most handsome man in the room."

CHAPTER 8

She now had a house full of family. For the first time in several years, there were sounds of movement in the dorment guest bedrooms across the hall. Sounds of laughter, of tears, of anger, of whispering and of normal conversation. In other words, Mowbray Estate was now alive and thriving with activity, and Lucy had never felt more eventful.

Lord and Lady Mowbray insisted on having their meals sent up to their rooms for the first two days, then out of the blue, decided to join Lucy on their third day of sunrise.

Horace II, his wife Marjory, and their three children came in together, followed by Felicity and Arthur in tow.

Lucy looked up shocked as each one pulled out a chair and took their seats. Slowly lowering her teacup, her eyes bounced from one to the other as they sat down quiet for a few seconds, then the two boys bent over and grabbed at the jam.

Horace II, stared down his two boys and barked, "Not yet, boys."

Lucy watched the boys stiffen up in disappointment. "You boys must be starving, go ahead, there's plenty," she instructed, bowing her head towards Horace II.

Horace II looked over at Lucy and declared, "Your household has been most obliging Madam, we are humbled by your continued hospitality and we extend our thanks and gratitude."

Lucy blinked back her surprise and then rested eyes on Arthur, "You are my family, Lord Mowbray, it is what your father would have done if he were alive."

Felicity lowered her eyes, "That is correct, Madam, it is what father would have done."

Lucy watched her smile and then rested eyes on Arthur again. He was avoiding eye contact with her and she wondered why. She looked across at Rebecca who had been seated all the way at the end. "Lady Rebecca, do you draw?"

Rebecca looked up from her food and then replied, "Why yes, I do."

Lucy smiled and then looked across at her mother, "There is a lovely room in the corner of the estate where the natural light is at its brightest where she can continue. I took the liberty of ordering canvas, paints, oils and brushes, if you do not mind."

Lady Mowbray smiled graciously, "No, Madam, I do not mind at all. Thank you so much for your hospitality, our comfort here has been most welcome."

Arthur was beside himself the moment he sat down. He had always cared for Lucy, more so than he cared to admit. Feelings for her that were buried deep were awakened by their coquettish conversations at the Frimley's. He would have had her in his bed years ago when she was a housemaid, but every time he would try to get her alone, his father beat him to the pursuit. *His father,* he thought, *the man he grew to hate was now her late husband.* Arthur looked across at Lucy who was probably wondering why he hadn't uttered a word to her since his advent. "Do you ride, Madam?" Arthur spoke up at last, wiping his mouth off with a cloth napkin.

Lucy gazed into his eyes, "I haven't ridden in a very long time."

"Would you care to ride with me this afternoon?" Arthur asked, waiting on her response.

Lucy gazed at Horace II first and then accepted, "I would love that, thank you."

It was a lovely day for a horseback ride and Lucy hadn't been on a horse since her husband had passed. The last time she did ride was when Horace and she rode together with the Frimley's, and she felt melancholy for those days gone by.

Riding to a patch of grass overlooking the mountains and hills, Lucy dismounted her horse and allowed him to graze while she took in the greenery and magnificent views of her own land.

Arthur pulled up beside her horse and dismounted his, and walked over to be by her side, "Did my father choose this land or did you?"

Lucy smiled and did not look at him straight away, "To be honest, I would like to say I did and take all the credit, but it was your father. He said he always admired the hills and mountains from this vantage point."

Arthur nodded his head, "Father always did have an eye for beauty."

Lucy turned to look at Arthur as he turned his head towards hers. He leered down at her and felt her chin lifting up … to what? *Oh dear Lord,* she wanted to *kiss him* and immediately disguised her intentions as she coughed and walked away.

Arthur stepped forward as well, "You know you have surprised my brother."

"In what way?" Lucy asked, still traipsing onwards.

Arthur continued to follow her lead, "He believed you would have truly cast him out. He quite expected to be rejected and to receive your retort."

Lucy halted and then spun around, insulted she spurt out, "Is that what you *all* believe? That I am some cold-hearted opportunist?"

Arthur shook his head, "My brother and my sister are very old-fashioned and believed our father would die a widower. Then *you* came along."

Lucy rolled her eyes and looked up at the blue sky, "Contrary to public opinion, I cared deeply for Horace—and I *do* miss him."

Arthur cocked his head and was injured by her statement, "I was off at Cambridge when he began courting you, I cannot tell you whether or not my father cared deeply for *you*."

"He did," Lucy supplied him. "Very much so, in fact, this land, the estate, everything he left me is proof how much he *loved* me."

Arthur circled his eyes around her face. The suns rays had shined brightly in and around her fiery red hair, and her bright blue eyes looked like two topaz stones. He did not know whether he should continue to debate her, or kiss her. He fought back his temptation to do the latter and uttered, "I can see why my father was so enamored by you."

Lucy bore into his hazel eyes and swallowed her lust for him, "How so?"

"I daresay, your beauty paired to your spirited countenance is quite irresistible," Arthur relayed, conquered by her passionate guise.

CHAPTER 9

*L*ucy bore into his hazel eyes, and the heat found there warmed her entire body and her face flushed. Turning away, she walked back towards her horse, "We must return."

Arthur stood his ground, "I am due back in Portsmouth tomorrow."

Lucy was about to mount but released the saddle pommel, "How long will you be gone?"

Arthur walked over to her horse and petted his neck and mane, "For about a month. I often stay in Portsmouth for work and take social calls while I am there. I should return in thirty days or so."

Lucy slowly shut her eyes and then gazed out towards the mountains. Inside she was hurting, it was painful to hear of his departure, but she knew he had business elsewhere. He was a working Gentleman, unlike his unemployed brother who just flittered about from one social engagement to the next. "I will miss your amiable company, Lord Mowbray."

Arthur knew he was walking on dangerous ground but his heart was bursting every which way, "Will you miss *me*?"

Lucy looked up into his eyes. The passion alone melted her resolve. "I will miss your amiable company," she repeated and whispered out in front of her.

"But *not* me?" Arthur asked plainly.

"What is it you would like me to admit?" Lucy asked, feeling her throat close up.

Arthur circled his eyes around her face, "Admit to what was felt during conversation at the Frimley's."

Lucy closed her eyes, and was about to get back up on her saddle, "This is wrong, it is immoral."

Arthur walked away from the horse and back over to her side, "What is immoral? Our friendship, or the possibility of becoming lovers? I know you feel it—this intense attraction that surrounds us both. We should be in *bed*, not on *horseback*."

Lucy lowered her head and dug her riding boot into the dirt, "I cannot do this to him. I cannot tarnish the memory of his good name."

"His good name?" Arthur laughed sickly, "Did you know he used to beat our mother?"

Lucy's face flushed with shock, "What?"

Arthur let go a snappish grin, "Yes, quite the chameleon my father was. When my brother and sister were younger, he used to beat them and call them names, he was a *horrid* man, and when I became of age and would not listen or cry or try to run away, he would turn his anger on our mother for attempting to protect me."

Lucy's mouth flew open wide, "He never once showed anger towards me, he was a *good* man."

Arthur stepped in closer and lifted up her chin, "Of course he was good to you, he expected you in his bed."

Lucy turned away from him, "Do not talk of this."

Arthur spun her around, his two hands on each shoulder, "You must know the truth about our father. Perhaps you will now understand why my brother and sister are so disagreeable with you."

Lucy tilted her head, "Let me go."

Arthur released her shoulders but did not step away from her, "You must know the beatings ended a week before she died."

Lucy blinked back her shock about the man who was once her husband. *Was Horace responsible for her death? How could he have done such a thing? What cruelty his children must have faced when they were younger. If they had had children of their own, would they have been subjected to the same torment?* It was no wonder they despised her so ... Horace had always treated her like a delicate rose. Lucy gazed over at the mountains then back at Arthur. He was so diverse from his father and yet, he was like him in every way. Just a virile, younger version of what she missed most. "We never argued," she softly admitted, then gazed up at him grimacing, "Your poor mother."

Arthur gazed up at the sky momentarily, "She was a good woman."

Lucy shook her head in agreement, "I thank you for this insight, Lord Mowbray."

Arthur could not take any more of the temptation to touch her. His prurient nature overflowed every inch of his pores. He let go a roguish grin, "There are other ways to show gratitude, my dear."

And there it was.

The invitation she so desperately searched for. Lucy gave him a gamine smile and he must have read her mind for the next thing she knew was him grabbing her body into his, and kissing her lips, softly at first, then ardently, as his tongue burst passed her brim, tasting her and sending her on the brink of desire. Lucy broke away from his lips and whispered, "There is a bedroom behind the library that no one is aware of."

"A secret bedroom?" Arthur whispered back.

"Will you meet me there?" Lucy asked, trying to keep hold of his ardor, "At midnight?"

Arthur bore into her eyes, "At midnight."

THE ROOM USED TO BE AN OFFICE UNTIL LUCY had it rebuilt for indiscretion. A bed, a nightstand, a rug and an oil lamp were all that was in there, and no one in her household knew about the secret room, no one but Mary.

Dressed in just a nightgown, Lucy waited for Arthur to come in through the library's secret door. She waited ten painstakingly minutes until the door open and closed.

Arthur was dressed in a long white shirt, pantaloons and no shoes, and stepped into her and grabbed her body to his in craze.

Kissing, necking, groping at one another's bodies, their urgency to get closer was apparent, as Lucy helped pull his shirt up over his head, as Arthur pulled down her nightgown so that they were both naked, and he picked her body up only to lie with her on the bed.

Over and across her form, he bent down over her breasts and buried his head on top of her chest, squeezing, and suckling her nipples; his lewd tongue up and around her mounds. His mouth trailed away from her skin up to her neck where he felt Lucy's hands roaming his backside in haste. Aiding her with what she wanted, he opened up her thighs with his knee and he gradually entered her crux, thick, hard and satisfying. Rocking to and fro, she pushed into his hips to receive all of him, continuing to caress him everywhere, as they reached climax in unison, breathing heavily at their joint endeavor only to come together again in a long impassioned kiss and replay the same conclusion throughout the night.

CHAPTER 10

By next morning, Arthur was gone.

Lucy did not want to believe that Arthur would truly leave but he set off to Portsmouth before sunrise. He made sure that she was asleep before he dressed, and packed his bags, the rotten scoundrel. Lucy was now soaking in a bath that Mary made for her minutes before.

Leaning up against the rim of the tub, Lucy closed her eyes and reimagined Arthur's carnal hunger and him on top of her; pounding between the core of her legs, sending her to rapture over and over again.

"More hot water?" Mary asked, standing over her nakedness.

Lucy opened her eyes and gazed up, "Yes, please."

Mary walked across to the pitcher she carried up and

then slowly walked over to pour the hot water at the base of Lucy's exposed legs. The water flowed passed her skin, up around her midriff and fully submerged Lucy's full breasts. "Lady Rebecca has asked to meet with you after breakfast," Mary relayed, taking a cloth and rubbing Lucy's back.

Lucy surged forward so that Mary could reach her lower, "She has? I wonder what it could entail."

Then silence.

"The younger left early this morning," Mary conveyed, biting down on her lower lip.

Lucy rolled her eyes up at her, "He did?"

Mary continued to bite down on her lower lip, "I overheard him tell his brother that he would be gone for more than a month and to write him if there was any news regarding Lavernham."

Lucy lowered her head, "Over a month? Are you sure that is what you heard?"

Mary grabbed the pitcher and submerged it into the water and was about to pour it over Lucy's head, "I am quite sure. Did he not tell you so when he left your bed?"

Lucy was just about to retort when Mary poured the hot water over her head. "Oh!" She cried out, wiping the water away from her eyes. "Why you wretch of a girl! So you know?"

Mary started to laugh, "Of course, I know. I must know everything there is to know about you if I am to be a *true* lady's maid. Your good health, your illnesses, your monthly flow, where you sleep and with *whom*."

Lucy splashed water up into her face, "You make me sound out to be some kind of barn creature."

"A sensual beast full of lust and desire. So, pray tell, how was he?" Mary asked plainly.

Lucy swished the water around with her hands, "Prurient, more so than the rest."

Mary rolled her eyes, "Oh how I envy you. The last time I lied down with a bloke, he finished before I could pull up my skirts."

Lucy began to laugh, "When was this?"

Mary gazed up at the ceiling, "Two months? Maybe three?"

Lucy continued to giggle, "And who was this *bloke*?"

Mary grinned, "One of your footmen."

Lucy shook her head, "Do not let Mrs. Thatchwood catch you, she might request his employment be terminated."

"We were discreet," Mary said with a smile. "Besides, I think he's lost interest in me."

"Or he could be very well embarrassed for concluding too soon," Lucy joked, standing up now to be wrapped in a towel.

Mary lowered her eyes down to her generous breasts, "Your nipples are swollen."

Lucy gazed down at her bosom, "He suckled me like a baby throughout the night."

Mary sighed, "Oh how I envy you."

Lucy gave her a smile and then walked to her bedroom in just her towel. Looking down at the black gown on top of her bed, she turned swiftly around to face Mary, "I'm done with mourning. I do not wish to feel sad anymore, especially on this day when I feel nothing *but* elation. I want to wear pink today."

"Has lust turned into love?" Mary asked, holding her silk robe open so Lucy could walk into it.

Lucy dropped her towel to the floor and took one arm and then wrapped herself around into the other, "I daresay, it has."

"Does he know you love him?" Mary asked, pulling Lucy's wet hair out from within the silk and drying her hair off with a towel.

"No," Lucy said, a little melancholy. "And I fear he will never know."

"Write him, maybe he will return your affections?" Mary quipped, brushing Lucy's hair that turned dark red from the water.

"To be truthful Mary, I do not know what his intentions are. I wanted him as badly as he wanted me,"

Lucy expressed, gazing at Mary's form in the reflection of the mirror. "What we shared was lust, not love, and Arthur may not hold affection for me."

Mary shook her head, "Maybe it is just lust you are feeling, let us wait a few days to see if the sentiment remains."

"Lady Rebecca, how are you getting on?" Lucy asked, entering the corner morning parlor where Rebecca had been painting.

She set her paint brush down and then gazed up at the ceiling, "There is not a more pleasant room to paint in. I cannot thank you enough Madame, you have made a tragedy more approachable."

Lucy walked in towards her and then lowered her eyes to the canvas where she was in the middle of painting. It was her husband, Lord Horace Mowbray, a wonderful likeness Rebecca had drawn from memory. *Why had she not seen it before? Arthur held the same nose and eyes as his father. Was it Horace that she truly missed?* "You are very talented," Lucy expressed, smiling back at her.

Rebecca tilted her head and raised her paintbrush up to the canvas, "I always liked my grandfather in red, do you not think it is too vulgar?"

Lucy eyed the red waistcoat she painted on his chest and down his belly, "No, I think it is perfect."

"Thank you, Madam," Rebecca accepted, smiling graciously at her.

"Do you know where your father might be?" Lucy asked next, looking out the windows.

"He is out walking the dogs, I believe," Rebecca said, sort of nonchalantly.

"Dogs?" Lucy laughed, "Where were those stashed away?"

Rebecca started to laugh as well, "Oh I do apologize, our footmen brought them yesterday, they required washing."

Lucy swallowed her smile and thought how wonderful it was to have an address full of family which included dogs now. She always wanted a dog and wondered why she never procured one.

CHAPTER 11

PORTSMOUTH

*A*rthur sat in his high office, overlooking the hustle and bustle of the going-ons of the wharf down below. Ships carrying cargo entered the harbor from the sea, men pulling trade crates off those ships, passengers gaining entrance and walking the planks, children, baby buggies, horses pulling wagons and hundreds of immigrants walking aimlessly about.

At the beginning of the Eighteenth Century, Portsmouth Dockyard continued to expand. New docks and warehouses were being built. A church dedicated to St. Anne was built in 1704. Rows of houses were built in the dockyard for senior officers who needed to be close to their work, and a naval academy for training naval officers was also opened in the dockyard in 1733.

Arthur had been working with the chief engineer

building the Portsmouth and Arundel Canal. The canal was being built across Portsea Island. The Portsmouth to Arundel canal would run just outside of town, locking on the southeastern shore where barges would be able to tow trade across the sea into Chichester Harbor, where the canal would begin again.

He was also a solicitor in the maritime court, exercising jurisdiction over all maritime contracts, torts, injuries and offenses. Shipowners owed a duty of reasonable safety to their passengers and workers. Consequently, passengers or workers who were injured aboard ships and barges brought about suits if they were injured ashore or onboard through the negligence of a third party. The passenger or worker did bear the burden of proving that the shipowner was negligent, but many did try and Arthur's services were in high demand. It was a worthy profession and Arthur sometimes dealt with the Royal Navy, and since he was the son of an Earl, gained passage easily through the ranks of officers.

IT CAME AS QUITE A SHOCK TO LORD HORACE Mowbray I, when his wife announced she was with child at forty-six. When most women were experiencing the change of life, Lady Mowbray was preparing the nursery.

Her older children, Horace II and Felicity were both in their early twenties, imagine her confusion when the doctor's told her she was pregnant with her third?

Arthur knew he might have been conceived out of *hate* rather than of *love* when he witnessed his father's anger towards his mother when he pushed her up against the wall when he was very small. **"*Control him,*"** were words embedded into his memory at five years old, and would later be firmly established by further abuse towards his sister, Felicity.

He was ten years old when his mother died. It was a sad day full of anguish and uncertainty. Her absence meant that there would be no more shelter from the anger-filled blows and thunderous rows he was accustomed to, and Arthur begged his older brother to help win favor of sending him to boarding school, and could not wait to get out of Lavernham and away from his father's brutish attitude.

Arthur would return home only for Christmas and on his father's birthday, and was shocked as each year went by, his father grew less and less infuriated. The passing of his mother meant wild child-like behavior, and Arthur was disturbed by his father's impropriety. Gossip throughout the house, learning from his sister that their father had been caught dallying with two or three of the housemaids. Women walking out of the back door in the wee hours of the morning, their father disappearing during family parties, and social gatherings that lasted till sunrise.

He could not blame his brother and sister having concerns over marrying Miss Lucy Gibbon, a *housemaid*. He remembered her first day working at Lavernham Manor. She was fifteen, from a poor family pressuring her to work to feed her debilitated parents. She knew nothing about cleaning an estate, but learned quickly or else she would be forced onto the streets to learn another profession.

Miss Lucy Gibbon started the same day as Miss Mary Hurndale, and between the two young maidens, Lucy outshined her coworker by her natural beauty and spark. Her fiery red hair was hard to miss, and when she entered the room to clean, men had always turned to look at her.

It had only been a few months at Lavernham when their paths first crossed. She was fifteen, he, twenty-one and leaving to school to study law. Her appearance was stunning, and he remembered following her around in the shadows while she completed her household duties. Once, he did try to start a conversation with her, but she was always too shy, and never looked up from her feather duster. He left her side, always feeling a wandering sentiment unmet. A yearning to get to know her never quite fulfilled until the day he learned that she was to wed his father. The pain he felt was unfamiliar, having never felt those feelings before, and Lucy looked absolutely beautiful on her wedding day, with her white wedding dress and long flowing veil; even then he felt the urge to be by her side and took that opportunity to kiss the bride. He wanted her more than he realized, and was disappointed in himself that he did not steal her away when he had the chance to do so.

But now, after tasting her, his quench for her skin would never be fully met. *He was in love with her,* he concluded … *must have always been in love with her* and was melancholy over the realization. His woe at present was of a personal nature, one that stemmed from bedding his father's *widow*.

His father's widow…

His father *had her* first…

He did not want to leave the following morning after their intimacy, but the reality of him bedding his father's widow felt like bile stuck in his throat.

How was he ever supposed to surmount this comprehension?

CHAPTER 12

MOWBRAY ESTATE

*L*ucy sat in her garden and pulled petals from a daisy. She yearned for Arthur daily, but was too prideful to write and tell him so.

It had been three weeks with no correspondence from him either, and it afflicted her that he would be so self-centered, and without rapport. She grabbed another flower, only this time a rose, and began plucking its velvety petals from its stem. Looking up she was takenback when she saw Horace II walking towards her. He stopped just a few feet away, and bowed his head at her presence.

"Madam, may I have a word?"

Lucy dropped the flower to one side and pointed towards the empty bench across from her, "Do sit down, Lord Mowbray."

Horace II gazed at the empty bench and took his seat. He cleared his throat before declaring, "I've received a letter from my architect indicating the rebuilding of Lavernham would take approximately ... three years to complete."

Lucy looked deep into his eyes, *was he serious?* "Three years, is he sure?"

Horace II shook his head, "Yes Madame, Lavernham was built in the 1702 and the materials used were old and decayed. He was surprised there wasn't a fire earlier."

Lucy cocked her head, "So have you located better lodgings?"

Horace II bit down on his tongue, "Why no Madam, it is why I came to see you."

Lucy dropped his eyes down the length of him. He was a proud man, by his attitude and his fashion. He did not look like his father at all and Lucy assumed he took more after their mother. With dark brown hair and almost black eyes, there wasn't a trait in his face that seemed amiable. "How long will you be staying then?"

Horace II sighed, "The full three years. I ask for continued hospitality."

Lucy turned away from him in that moment, and thought about Arthur. If his brother heard from him or not and wondered if he had written him a letter indicating his wishes to stay for another three years. "And Arthur? Does he know?"

Horace II squinted his eyes at her, "No Madam, I have yet to write my brother. My writing him depended on your reply."

Lucy gazed down at her satin shoes, "Oh I see."

"If you are displeased by us continuing to lodge here, we shall have no other choice but to inquire on lodgings elsewhere," Horace II said quickly, treading the unease.

Lucy folded her hands on her lap, "Lord Mowbray, your actions have never been favorable towards me. You and your sister have always treated me as an outcast."

Horace II lowered his eyes, "I apologize for our behavior, Madam, my sister and I have always been cautious with the company my father kept."

Lucy tilted her head, "Elaborate, Lord Mowbray. You cannot set a bomb down without expecting it to explode."

Horace II grinned at her analogy, "There were many others before you, Madam."

Lucy gazed deep into his eyes. His admission was startling, but it did not injure her like she thought it would. "How many?"

"Many," Horace II admitted, continuing to grin.

Just then Lucy fathomed why he and his sister were wary of her marriage to their father. They believed she was just *one* of *many*. "He did love me," she softly voiced, eyeing the rose next to her on the bench.

Horace II dropped his eyes to the petals she had already pulled out, "Did my father confess such sentiment?"

Lucy wondered why it was so important to know the truth, "Yes, he did. On more than one occasion, Lord Mowbray, your father expressed his devotion."

"Because he hated our mother," Horace II replied hastily, "my sister and I always believed he despised *women* in general, and did not wish to see happiness in the eyes of the softer sex."

"How so, Lord Mowbray when he has shown me great adoration with leaving me the very ground you now stand on?" Lucy asked, raising her head proudly.

"Did you know my sister was once engaged to the Marquess of Bisham?" He asked, quizzing her to an extent of how much his father did adore her.

Lucy straitened her head, "No, Lord Mowbray, I did not."

Horace II let go a roguish grin, "On her wedding day, the Marquess caught our father in a compromised position with *his* sister."

Lucy slowly closed her eyes and lowered her head, "Oh, how dreadful."

"The Marquess refused to marry Felicity, leaving her in tears and repudiated by future suitors," he added, standing back up to his feet. "Did you not wonder why a beautiful woman like my sister never married?"

Lady Felicity Mowbray was once very beautiful, it was true, but as the years passed, her dark brown hair was replaced by gray, and her smoldering dark eyes grew dim and weary. Lucy watched him as he began to walk back and forth before her, "Do sit down, Lord Mowbray, you are making me dizzy."

Horace II laughed at her straight-forwardness, "I cannot sit any longer, Madame! Perhaps this conversation is long over due."

Lucy now stood up from *her* seated position, "Then say what you have to say and get on with it."

Lord Mowbray lifted up his chin, "You and your *beguiling* ways."

Lucy began to chortle, "Beguiling? You mean my affinity with your sex?"

"Yes, Madam, and I am assuming you have *beguiled* my brother right back to Portsmouth as well," he remarked, saluting his arm in the air.

"What are you implying, Sir?" Lucy asked, with her hands on her hips.

Lord Mowbray dropped his eyes down to her bodice and her ample bosom, "That you have had your way with him, and he with you, otherwise my brother would have *stayed*."

CHAPTER 13

Lucy had been covertly staring at Lady Felicity Mowbray from across the meadow. Lucy had been sitting on a blanket in the middle of the grasses, and Felicity was sitting in the garden by the rose bushes towards the house.

Lucy brought to mind what Lord Mowbray confessed to her the other day during their sordid conversation. That he and his sister both believed that she was an opportunist and beguiled their father. *His statement could be further from the truth! Lord Mowbray plundered her!* He was the one who constantly sought her out, pleaded for her undivided attention—it was never the other way around. *Who beguiled who?* She did not seduce *him*—he seduced *her* with his wealth, his charming ways, and his promise to take care of her always. Then she thought of Arthur and what his brother said about him having had his way with her, and she with him. *It was the truth,* this much she knew for sure! *Would he have stayed otherwise?* She never wanted another man like she did Arthur. *She was in love with him, deeply in love with him, and wondered how she was ever going to forget him.*

Lucy sat on her hip and raised her eyes towards Felicity again. She had been playing with a rose she pulled off minutes before. She was still very beautiful. Time had only wrinkled the lines around her eyes and the corners of her lips, but she was still in good health and pleasant on the eyes. Lucy thought about several bachelors that she's met over the years that might be searching for a companion for life. A man who was not seeking a brood mare for heirs, but a lasting friendship, and warm arms during the cold winter nights.

She was just about to stand up on her feet to start up a conversation with her, when she noticed Felicity had been walking towards her locale.

Within reaching the blanket, Felicity extended out her hand and asked, "May I join you?"

Lucy gazed up at her cordiality and replied, "Please do."

Felicity sat down on the blanket beside her and bent

her legs to the side, gazing out towards the hills beyond and said, "This is a lovely place. I can see why my father built this sanctuary for you."

Lucy instantly recalled what her brother relayed to her, "Your father was most generous towards me, Lady Felicity, and his adoration was oftentimes displayed through his gifts."

Felicity smiled, "I know, Madam. I can now fathom why."

Lucy then lowered her head and thought about her engagement to the Marquess of Bisham, "Would you mind if I hosted a dinner party next week for a few of my friends in your honor? Most assuredly, your brother is invited as well."

Felicity gazed into her eyes, "Who, may I ask will you be extending an invitation?"

Lucy swallowed and wondered why she was so curious, "Mr. Bishop, Mr. Ainsworth, Baron Huntsworth, the Earl of Wexhall, and Mr. and Mrs. Frimley."

Felicity let go a chuckle, "That is quite the guest list!"

Lucy began to coyly finger the rim of her dress, "Do you not approve?"

Felicity adjusted her seated position on the blanket,

"No, I do approve. I forgot what excitement felt like from the possibility of being matched. You surprised me, that is all."

Lucy reached over and grabbed at her hand, "Any one of those Gentlemen would keep you in the highest regard, I do assure you."

Felicity lowered her eyes to her hand around hers, "The Marquess of Bisham now has six children. I often wondered what life would have been if only my father—"

Lucy shook her head, "Do you not live in the past, Lady Felicity, only regret exists there."

Felicity squeezed her hand and gave her half a smile, "I daresay, you are wise beyond your years."

"I thank you for the compliment," Lucy said with a smile.

"I have underestimated your hospitality, Madam and I do apologize for my past indiscretions," Lady Felicity said next. "You have shown my brother and I a great kindness, and we do not know how to ever repay you."

Lucy gave her a smile, "Your continued harmony and rapport is all the repayment I shall ever seek."

Felicity fought back tears, "Did my brother let it be known that Lavernham will take three years to rebuild?"

Lucy nodded her head, yes and was thrilled that their bridge of friendship was now on the mend.

Felicity then gazed out towards the hills, "Has Arthur written you?"

Lucy looked deep into her eyes. She felt an unknown sting pierce her heart in that moment, "No, he has not."

Felicity nodded her own head, "With Lavernham being rebuilt, it is probably best that he remains in Portsmouth. He has a townhome there and I believe he will be heading off to France soon. He is sort of a wayward."

Lucy could not believe her ears! "France? Whatever for?"

Felicity noted the difference in Lucy's worried voice, "He has accepted a position in Le Harve after the Arundel Canal has been built. Did he not mention this on his departure?"

"No, he did not," Lucy replied quickly, feeling injured by her decree.

"The scamp," she let go, "always a mystery that boy is."

Lucy fought back her tears, "I daresay he is."

Felicity leaned back and pulled some grass out by her hand, "I do wish Arthur would end his refusal on any match my brother introduces. He has batted down several fine young ladies, all of which are from good family, he's even avoided the marriage mart while he stays in London! The rascally scamp."

Lucy closed her eyes and appeared sick in that moment and felt like throwing up. Imagining Arthur with anyone other than herself was making her ill beyond repair.

CHAPTER 14

Lucy sat alone on a chair, and gazed across at Lady Felicity conversing with the Gentleman at her dinner party. They were all situated in the drinking parlor before dinner, with every man hovering over her trying to gain her sole attention. Mr. Ainsworth was a wealthy tailor in his early forties; never married, he was the quintessential bachelor and would make a perfect match. Mr. Bishop, a widower, in his late forties owned several iron mills, Baron Huntsworth, a shy, amiable Gentry, and the Earl of Wexhall, too good for anyone, but titled to match hers.

Mr. Ainsworth in particular, seemed charmed by Felicity's outer appearance and his eyes lit up each and every time she smiled, until the Earl of Wexhall stood between them, and stole her attention away.

Mr. Ainsworth seemed tortured, and walked away with his head bent down. Lucy stood up immediately, and went to rescue him, "Why Mr. Ainsworth, I do not believe I have ever seen you give up so easily during a hunt."

Mr. Ainsworth circled his eyes towards Lady Felicity, "She is enchanting, where have you been hiding her?"

"Lost near London, I'm afraid," Lucy quipped, sipping her wine, "You find favor in her?"

"Very much so," he added, "she is a widow?"

Lucy shook her head, "No, Mr. Ainsworth, she has never been married."

"Never married you say?" He asked, taken-back. "Surely there have been engagements?"

"Yes," Lucy said quickly, "to the Marquess of Bisham."

He raised an eyebrow, "Know of the name, not of the man."

Just then, Mr. Bishop joined them forming a circle, "Lovely party, Madam, Lord and Lady Mowbray seem genuine."

Lucy surveyed the room and pin-pointed the Earl and his wife, "Yes, once you get to know them."

Mr. Bishop smiled, "Any other hopefuls, my dear? This one seems quite taken with Ainsworth here."

"Do you believe so?" Mr. Ainsworth asked, turning

back to take another look at the enchantress. She had been eyeing his locale ever since he left.

"Poor bastard—he does not stand a chance," Mr. Bishop relayed, drinking the rest of his Port, and shaking his head at the Earl of Wexhall trying to gain Felicity's attention, as her eyes glued themselves to Mr. Ainsworth as he left their side.

"How are you?" Lucy asked, genuinely.

Mr. Bishop let go a small smile before he sipped his Port, "Well, thank you. I was surprised to receive your invitation ... how are you these days?"

Lucy gazed around the room, "As well as can be with family now to claim."

"Hold onto them," Mr. Bishop relayed, "loneliness can be poison to one's mind."

Lucy gazed up at him and remembered the last time she was in his arms. Since then, they had written letters to keep acquainted, and she did cherish their familiar friendship. *What else could she help him with?* "Are you looking for someone like Lady Felicity or someone younger?" Lucy asked, safely.

Mr. Bishop chuckled and then turned to look down into Lucy's beautiful blue eyes, "I've been alone these twenty years now since my Charlotte died, any companionship would be most welcome."

Lucy smiled, "Does the women require a title? Or of good family?"

Mr. Bishop grinned at her questioning, "If I did not know any better, Madam, I would say you are trying to *match* me."

Lucy grinned at his reply, "You would be correct, Mr. Bishop."

He let go another roguish grin and gazed around at the party, "She must be amiable."

Lucy gathered in his straightforwardness, "A lady's maid?"

Mr. Bishop cocked his head, "Know of one?"

Lucy smiled wide, "I do indeed." She left Mr. Bishop's side only to walk away to speak to Felicity. She was barely a few feet away from her presence when Lord Mowbray stepped into her view.

"Madam," he let go sternly, "I seem to be thanking you more than once these days." He turned to gaze at his sister who seemed joyously gratified.

Lucy let go a small smile, "Yes, Lord Mowbray but there is no need. I was glad my acquaintances with your sex turned out to be beneficial."

Lord Mowbray frowned at her comment, "Another bold remark. I daresay, Madam you are loose with your tongue."

"It is the *Regency* Lord Mowbray, do loosen your

necktie," Lucy requested sharply, as she walked away to grab Felicity by her arm, and into a corner for a chit-chat like two giggling schoolgirls. "I daresay, Lady Felicity the smile on your face may be mistaken for enjoying the excess?"

Felicity cupped her gloved hand around Lucy's chin, "I cannot remember the last time I was *this* happy."

Lucy wrapped her own gloved hand around hers, "Mr. Ainsworth has expressed his interest in multitude."

Felicity's eyes grew wide, "He has?"

Lucy recalled how large he was in his lower extremities, and thought how fortunate Felicity would be during their intimacy. She nodded her head, "Yes, indeed. Does this make you happy?"

"Very much so, Madam, I daresay I find him the most attractive," Felicity let go turning her head towards Mr. Ainsworth now chatting with her brother.

"Dinner is served," Mr. Dunbar pronounced, with a short bow.

"I will make sure you sit by him," Lucy whispered, placing down her wine glass, and heading out the door with Mr. Dunbar towards the dining room, where a magnificent display of opulence had been set up.

She walked in first only to close the double doors behind her. Scampering over to the table, she shuffled around the name cards from the Earl of Wexhall, to Mr. Ainsworth to be seated next to Felicity.

She then ran her eyes down the length of the table. *Oh how she wished Arthur could be there!* Ambling over to the double doors, she flung them open and announced, "Fish this evening, hope everyone enjoys the grilled mackerel with beetroot."

Mr. Bishop smoothed down his waistcoat, "Oh, I do enjoy a good grill."

Lucy smiled and watched everyone stand over their name cards. "Do sit down," she instructed, waving her hand out in front of her. She took her own seat and eyed Mr. Dunbar to send in the food. She was all smiles up until the main course was set out on the table. Silver trays filled with round lifeless eyes of several mackerel staring back at her.

All at once she felt *ill*.

The pungent smell of fish filled the entire room.

Lucy whipped her hand over her mouth and was about to throw up. She scuffled to her feet and darted out of the dining room only to vomit in the nearest vase she could find.

CHAPTER 15

PORTSMOUTH

*A*rthur stared down at the figures in the accounting book; it was money that Lavernham needed to rebuild. After the war, the prices of stone and lumber became inflated, with construction costs three times more over than what they were before the battle—with his brother's income, his sister's dowry, and what was left of his inheritance, how were they going to afford to rebuild?

He closed his eyes and instantly thought of Lucy. With her fiery red hair, blue eyes, and milky white skin. Freckles in secret places he enjoyed bussing throughout the night. The warmth between her legs, her thin waist leading up to her twin peaks that his tongue and mouth couldn't quite set free.

He *missed* her.

He was so deeply in love with her he could not see straight. It had been four long months since he touched her, and he knew that any more time passed between them would be excruciating.

He quickly grabbed a fountain pen and a sheet of paper and began to write her a love letter. *What would he say? How should he express his undying love? Would she leave the comfort of her home to travel to see him? Would she want to hear from him after not hearing from him for so long?*

My Darling Lucy,

My sincere apologies for not having written sooner...

"You have not written to me," he heard a voice say, "not once."

Arthur raised his eyes to the sound and received a jolt he hadn't quite counted on. *Lucy,* in the flesh ... in a long green carrick, and feathered brown hat. *She was here? She journeyed all this way?* His heart pounded recklessly at the sight of her. "What a pleasant surprise," he let go, smiling and setting down his pen.

Lucy was not amused. She and Mary travelled several days to Portsmouth, just to arrive amongst the filth and impoverished conditions. *How could he live and work here?*

Why did he not prefer the greenery and fresh smells of the countryside and of Mowbray Estate? Lucy was ill again the moment she set foot on the muddy terrain. Vomiting in the nearest barrel she could find, she threw up continuously after the smells of urine filled the air. "Why did you not tell me of your employment in Le Harve?"

Arthur tried to collect his thoughts. *When did he tell her about Le Harve? He did not mention his new assignment to anyone other than...* "Here now," he quipped, walking over to her but keeping his distance. He still wasn't sure why she came all this way. "I would have told you," he expressed, "if I had stayed longer at the Estate."

Lucy walked into his cramped office and gazed out the window and down at the hustle and bustle of the going-ons by the wharf. "Why did you leave?"

Arthur thought it was a trick question, "Why?"

Lucy continued to look out the window, "Why did you leave when you knew I needed you?"

Arthur continued to look at her backside, she was wearing a cream-colored dress under her carrick, and no longer wearing black. *How the devil was he supposed to know she needed him?* "You did not write to me to divulge this need."

Lucy shook her head in anger, "Do not be clever."

"Then how shall I be?" Arthur asked, wondering why she was acting this way. "You did not write to *me*."

Lucy closed her eyes, and swallowed her fiery pride, "Because I did not believe you wanted to *hear* from me."

Arthur shook his head, "Not true, I have missed you—painstakingly, *arduously*, missed you. Look there, on my writing desk—I was writing to you the very moment you walked back into my life!"

Lucy fought back her tears and slowly walked over to his desk. Eyeing the first words that began the letter *"My Darling Lucy"*, she cupped her gloved hands over her mouth and burst into tears.

Arthur now sprung forward and gathered her body into his. He wrapped his arms around her and hugged her body close. "I thought about writing you," he whispered by her ear, "many times in fact. But each and every time I thought maybe you did not want to hear from me."

Lucy pushed his warmth away, "How could you believe so? What we had shared, what we had expressed towards one another—how could that be imagined as repudiation?"

Arthur leaned in and gave her a kiss on her cheek, "My apologies, but the realization of what happened between us had me in constant turmoil with myself."

Lucy nodded her head, "I do understand, I do. I too have met unrest since your departure."

"Our joining has been unconventional to say the least," Arthur admitted, closing his eyes.

Lucy closed her own and felt safe within his arms, she was upset the moment she walked up the two staircases to get to his office on the third floor, but now she was just tired, and so glad to see him. All her anger melted at the sight of him dressed in dark gray, "I daresay, it has."

All at once, Arthur brought his hands up around her face and asked, "I love you Lucy, will you marry me?"

Lucy's mouth flew open wide, it was unexpected. Everything that had happened so far was so … *unexpected*. She smiled and replied, "Yes, Arthur, I will marry you."

Arthur smiled and leaned in to expect a kiss, but she pushed his lips away. *Was she mad?*

"First," Lucy expressed, holding both his hands in hers, "Decisions have been made which must be liberated at once."

Arthur raised an eyebrow, "Do tell."

Lucy leaned in and gave him that kiss, "I love you Arthur, and I cannot wait to be your wife and to wake up in your arms."

Arthur tilted his head. "I hear the hesitation in your voice," he said, leaning backward.

Lucy lifted up her chin, "You and your family will live at Mowbray and tear down Lavernham and sell the land."

Arthur tilted his head again, "That could work."

"Lady Felicity is set to marry Mr. Ainsworth *tomorrow*, and they are launching back to Dorking," she quickly uttered, feeling queasy all of a sudden. She hesitated and brought her gloved hand up over her mouth.

Arthur noted her displeasure and asked, "Darling, are you ill?"

Lucy wiped another tear of joy that had fallen from her eye, "Will you love me when I am fat and swollen?"

Arthur grinned at her morbidness, "In sickness and in health, of course darling Lucy, what is wrong?"

Lucy smiled and then confessed, "Good, because we are having a baby."

Arthur's eyes grew wide with shock, "A baby? Are you sure?"

"Most assuredly," Lucy nodded, as he grabbed her into him to swing her body around in seventh heaven.

A baby is what she *desired*, what she always *wanted*, and now her dream is … *fulfilled*.

THE SURPRISE HEIR

BY TRISHA FUENTES

In the charming era of Regency England, a tale of unexpected love and enduring destinies unfolds. **Edmund Gallagher**, a distant relative to the prestigious Lord of Langston Hall, lives a modest life far removed from the grandeur of his noble kin. His childhood memories of Langston Hall are few, but one delightful memory of climbing a treehouse with the young lord, **Rupert Hargrove**, continues to warm his heart through the years.

Now, decades later, Rupert, hailed as the dashing heir to Langston Hall, is poised to marry the impeccable Miss Abigail

Stronghold, securing his personal happiness and a prosperous future for the estate. However, just as wedding bells are to ring, an unforeseen tragedy befalls Rupert, turning Langston Hall upside down.

Equally entrapped by societal expectations and her burgeoning feelings, Miss Stronghold also finds herself at a crossroads. With the stability of Langston Hall and the future of its inhabitants uncertain, will Edmund and Abigail confront the dictates of their class and follow their hearts, or will they forsake personal happiness for the sake of tradition and duty?

This Regency romance weaves a compelling story of love, loss, and the choices that define us.

The Thunderbolt Series - Book 1

Ebook & Paperback

LOVE IN WINTER

LOVE LOST IN THE SEASON? SEARCHING FOR A WARM EMBRACE

Is Lady Alicia destined for a loveless marriage or a life on the shelf?

Follow Lady Alicia Henley's plight as societal pressures force her into the London Season. At twenty-five, she's adept at dodging suitors and yearns for something more than a preordained match.

But as the season closes and options dwindle, a drastic choice presents itself.

Will she settle for a loveless union or embark on a daring adventure across the sea?

The Caribbean beckons with the promise of sunshine and perhaps love.

Dive into a captivating tale of defying expectations and finding love in the most unexpected places.

Love in Winter is perfect for readers who adore:

- Regency Romance with a Twist
- Strong Female Leads Who Break the Mold
- Exotic Adventures that Heat Up the Pages

Escape the Ballroom and Discover Where True Love Waits!

A Regency Standalone Novella

Ebook & Paperback

ABOUT TRISHA

Hey, it's Trish...

I'm a Romance Author of 34+ books, plus an Indie Book Publisher of 48+ Pen Name Authors.

I've been writing romance with a whole lot of heat lately. I love to write fun, fast romances with witty leading ladies getting that gorgeous, sexy, yet lovable guy that doesn't take months to finish. Happily Ever After with a little bit of love angst in between. Whether you yearn for Historical or Modern, I always have a story for you!

Rejoice, Romance Reader...

For upcoming releases, book news, and other goodies, subscribe to my Newsletter!
https://mailchi.mp/567874a61a56/aab-landing-page

- instagram.com/authortrish
- amazon.com/Trisha-Fuentes/e/B002BME1MI
- facebook.com/booksbyTrish
- youtube.com/theardentartist

ALSO BY TRISHA FUENTES

✽ **Modern Romance** ✽

A Sacrifice Play

Faded Dreams

Never Say Forever

✽ **Historical** ✽

The Anzan Heir

Magnet & Steele

The Relentless Rogue

One Starry Night

In The Moonlight With You

Captivating the Captain

The Merry Widow

Unrequited Love

The Summer Romance of the Duke

✱ Series ✱

HOLLINGER

Dare To Love - Book 1

A Matchless Match - Book 2

Arrogance & Conceit - Book 3

Impropriety - Book 4

SERVICE • DAUGHTER

The Steward's Daughter - Book 1

The Cook's Daughter - Book 2

The Curator's Daughter - Book 3

THUNDERBOLT

The Surprise Heir - Book 1

A Dance of Deception - Book 2

Win the Heart of a Duchess - Book 3

OBSESSION

Unsuitable Obsession - Part One

Broken Obsession - Part Two

ESCAPE

Swept Away - Book 1

Fire & Rescue - Book 2

The Domain King - Book 3

AGE · GAP · ROMANCE

Whispers of Yesterday - Book 1

His Encore, Her Ecstasy - Book 2

Against the Wind - Book 3

www.ingramcontent.com/pod-product-compliance
Lightning Source LLC
LaVergne TN
LVHW010550070526
838199LV00063BA/4928